№26

№2

№39

№35

Backyard

BUGS

text and photographs by
ROBIN KITTRELL LAUGHLIN
foreword by
Sue Hubbell

CHRONICLE BOOKS
SAN FRANCISCO

THIS BOOK IS DEDICATED TO MY MOTHER, *Vivienne*.

Quote from "Speaking of Books and Life" by J. Donald Adams ©1953
by The New York Times Company. Reprinted by permission.

"Cheek to Cheek" from *Cheek to Cheek* by Jo Harvey Allen ©1995
by Jo Harvey Allen. Reprinted with permission of Duck Down Press, Nevada.

Excerpt from *Pilgrim at Tinker Creek* by Annie Dillard ©1974 by Annie Dillard.
Reprinted by permission of HarperCollins Publishers, Inc.

Printed in Hong Kong.
Library of Congress Cataloging-in-Publication Data:
Laughlin, Robin Kittrell.
Backyard Bugs / text and photographs by Robin Kittrell Laughlin.
p. cm.
ISBN 0-8118-0907-2
1. Arthropoda.   2. Arthropoda—Pictorial works.   I. Title.
QL434.14.L38   1996
595' .2' 0222—dc20   95-21386
CIP

Book and cover design: Kurt D. Hollomon
Composition: Cat Arnes
Cover photograph: Robin Kittrell Laughlin

Distributed in Canada by Raincoast Books,
8680 Cambie Street, Vancouver BC V6P 6M9

10 9 8 7 6 5 4 3 2 1

Chronicle Books
275 Fifth Street
San Francisco, CA 94103

Table of  contents

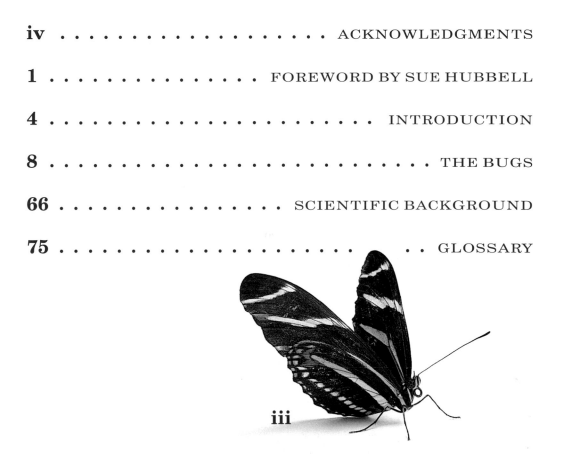

iii

acknowledgments

FIRST OF ALL, this book would not have gotten off the ground without Karen Silver's unflagging belief in the attractiveness of bugs. As my editor, she held my hand while I did things I never knew I was capable of. I could not have photographed and written about this varied a group of bugs without the generosity of my friends. Jane Fonda and Ted Turner made their ranches in New Mexico, Florida, and Montana available to me. Jane acted as my early editor, helping me to organize and distill my thoughts on paper. Danielle Gothie helped with my computer skills, and helped fine-tune my writing. Jane and Jimmy Buffett invited me to Shelter Island. My mother's place in Texas had plenty of bugs. Carol Anthony encouraged me to be myself in the writing process and helped with the design concept.

I AM ALSO GRATEFUL to those individuals who looked for bugs with me or on their own: Vivienne Wilson, Lisa Laughlin Boyd, Susy, Philip, and Thomas Duggins, Cary

Johnston, Vivienne Binnie, Juliana Seeligson, Eddie Wilson, Willie Reed, Eddie Lee Jones, Betty Jean Howell, Eloise Green, Jean Pagliuso, Mary Alice Palmer, Janie Dobrott, George Richards, Jey and Brian Wimberly, Donna Duke, Susan, Erin, Spencer, Brendan, and Chris Tolley, Tom Waddell, Karen Averitt, Chris Francis, Tom Rohrkaste, Lynn and Peter Coneway, Daphne and Martin Wood, Denise Lynch, and Kathryn Walker, who also inspired me to search for quotes about bugs.

HELP IN THE IDENTIFICATION PROCESS came from Linda Weiner, Steve Cary, Dick Fagerlund, Sandra Brantley, David Lightfoot, and Will Lanier. Barbara Malone at the Los Angeles Public Library helped me find great quotes about bugs.

Because we have them, we tend to think well of backbones, and so the animal world has been divided up by those people who think about that sort of thing into two great groupings: the vertebrates, animals with backbones, and the invertebrates, animals without backbones. There are a great many more of the latter than the former. Invertebrates are also much more important in maintaining a well-regulated planet of the sort we like than are vertebrates. If all of us animals with backbones were magicked away one day, the earth would tick along pretty much as it has been, but if animals without backbones disappeared, the rest of us would find our food chains breaking apart, our crops dying, the world filling up with waste and refuse, disease spreading without check, and we, too, would soon be eliminated from the planet. E. O. Wilson, the ant specialist and student of social insect behavior, has called invertebrates "the little things that run the world."

Invertebrates come in a dizzying array of animal life and form: starfish and sow bugs and sphinx moths and giant squid and snails and spiders and sea urchins and swallowtail butterflies and segmented worms and sponges . . . well, you get the idea. Small invertebrates, the ones we seldom eat and that crawl, fly, hop, and skitter, we usually lump together and call "bugs." People who aren't entomologists are sometimes worried about using that word around serious scientists. They are afraid that it is a little slangy, not Latinate enough to be an entomological term. Technically they are right because only one of the zoological orders of the class Insecta is called True Bugs: the Hemiptera. It includes such animals as water striders, squash bugs, and eastern toe-biters. But it is okay to use the word "bug" when we talk about all those other little guys; even entomologists do it when they are being informal. For we need a word that includes more than just insects, that encompasses all those creeping and flying and hopping bits of life, even if they represent, in a classificatory way, vastly different animals from a variety of entomological groupings. In this book you will meet a lot of bugs. Most of them are insects, members of the biological class Insecta, but others—the rolybugs, daddy longlegs, mites, spiders, and the vinegarone—belong to other classes and are as different, taxonomically speaking, as we (class Mammalia) are from birds (class Aves).

In my experience, youngsters who have not absorbed the current popular American notion that bugs are bad are fascinated with them. And so are adults who have shaken free from that notion. In truth, of all the millions of species of bugs, very

1

few are "bad" from a human standpoint. Some can sting or bite us and make us sick, some others like the same things we do—our food, our houses, our clothes—and are thus pests by our definition. But many are helpful to humans: honeybees pollinate our crops and also make us something tasty to eat. Many wasps feed to their young huge numbers of caterpillars that would harm our fruit trees. Beetles cart away our wastes. Ladybugs, golden lacewings, and a host of other predator bugs are sold to farmers and gardeners for biological pest control. Silkworm larvae spin the thread that makes one of our most elegant and prized fabrics. Butterflies are beautiful even to bug-haters.

The vast majority of bugs, however, neither help nor harm us. They are as indifferent to us and our ways as we are indifferent to them and the way they live their lives. Because research money is limited, most of it goes towards learning about bugs that are either harmful or beneficial to humans, while the indifferent bugs are little-studied. Many of them exist unknown and unnamed. Entomologists suspect that huge numbers of them remain undiscovered. And even among those that have been identified and "described," which is the entomologists' term for those animals that have been tucked into the classificatory scheme, little is known. In addition to the assigned name and physical description, perhaps an entomologist would add a note about the place the creature was found; at best its development from its eggish beginnings to adulthood may have been teased out by some patient watcher. But the intricacies of its biology, its behavior, its interrelationship with others of its kind, or its ways of getting along with the rest of bugdom and the greater world are most often unknown. As a result, when we humans interfere with their lives by destroying their surroundings or otherwise fiddling with the world, the effect of our fiddling, short- or long-term, is a surprise to us.

The ways bugs have of getting by in the world based on a biology so different from ours is a delight and, often, a puzzle. Therein lies a part of their fascination and attractiveness. They are mysterious animals. Children and the rest of us who have never quite grown up find that differentness, otherness, and mystery engaging in an intellectual sense, but also in another, nearly ineffable, way. It is, I suspect, part and parcel of our relationship to the rest of the natural world. C. S. Lewis phrased it elegantly when he wrote of our "yearning for other bloods." Lewis Thomas was getting at the same thing when he wrote "I am coded, somehow, for otters and beavers." E. O. Wilson has developed this notion in his 1984 book, *Biofilia,* and further explored it in a 1993 book he edited, *The Biofilia Hypothesis.* "Biofilia," a coinage, is defined by Wilson as "the innately emotional affiliation of **2** human beings to other living organisms." Wilson wonders whether biofilia might not be the basis for a conservation ethic. We became human and thrived in a world constituted in a certain way, chemically, botanically, zoologically. He suspects that as we, an upstart species only a couple of million years old at most (compared, say, to the insects, many of which have been around for about 400 million years), alter the atmosphere, land, and water of what was our own primeval world and extinguish species that were there when we first came into being—we do so at our own peril. "What," asks Wilson, "will happen to the human psyche as such a defining part of the human evolutionary experience is diminished or eroded?"

Another part of the appeal that bugs have for us, one that may be rooted in the first, however, is simply aesthetic. Everyone loves butterflies for their beauty, but all entomologists I have ever known or interviewed regard the subjects of their study as objects of loveliness. I once asked a woman mayfly expert how she had selected that particular insect for a lifetime of study. She replied, "They are such beautiful insects." An entomologist friend of mine once invited me to look closer at a tiny moth, undistinguished and dun-colored to the naked eye. Under his microscope it revealed itself, shimmering and gleaming, golden, decked out in all its mothly splendor. A goldsmith would have been impressed by its exquisiteness, as I was. I know several artists who use bugs as a basis for their artwork. One artist takes the themes of his sculptures from scanned electron microscope photos of honeybees and honeybee body parts. Natural form is at the base of our idea of beauty, and by altering the size of the real image—either by enlarging it through the scanning electron microscope, a regular microscope, a hand lens, or, as here in Robin Laughlin's handsome book, through artful photographic enlargement—the image becomes pure form to our eyes. Isolating the animal from its everyday background, as Laughlin has done, allows us to concentrate further on form, but also on color, dimension, and grace of body structure. We must be grateful for the perceptive and understanding eye of this exceptional photographer, who brings a generous beauty to our own eyes.

— *Sue Hubbell*

"Let us not forget that they preceded us by millions of years. They have an incomparably more ancient past, an incomparably greater experience. In the matter of time we are, from their point of view, the last comers, almost infants in swaddling clothes. Are we to declare them to be less intelligent than ourselves? ... Their intellectual efforts, like those of the great sages of the East, have taken a different direction — that is all. If they have not, like ourselves, advanced in mechanical methods and the exploitation of natural forces, the reason is simply that they had no need to; that, being endowed with a muscular strength two or three hundred times greater than our own, this strength sufficed, and required no artificial support or increase. It is also no less certain that they possess powers and senses of which we can form no conception ... "

—THE LIFE OF THE WHITE ANT, *Maurice Maeterlinck*
(TRANSLATED BY ALFRED SUTRO)

I suppose my interest in bugs began when I was a child. As a tomboy, I spent time alone, exploring a creek near my house. Outdoors I found relief from the oppression I felt indoors, from the constraints of being a child. Time passed more slowly, maybe because, as a child, I noticed small things, looked at details. Bugs were closer to my eye level then, they were friendly, for the most part, and they tickled. I guess there were fewer extraneous aspects of life to worry about, certainly no errands to run. I was not worried about the past or the future, so I could be totally present in the moment.

My house in northern New Mexico is a quiet refuge at the end of a road. It has always been a place where I could clear my head and feel unfettered. But lately I have allowed myself to be taken over by that busyness that prevents one from slowing down, from allowing empty chunks of time in which to just look and listen and feel. Working on this book mercifully took me out of the realm of social obligations and errands, and back into the marvelous world of childlike wonder and discovery.

I photographed the bugs indoors, at my own pace. I usually

4

put my subject in the refrigerator for a few minutes before taking its picture, to slow it down. Sometimes I had to repeat the process four or five times before I got a shot that satisfied me. This quick-chill was the most efficient, noninvasive means of getting the bugs to pose, since it was of paramount importance to me to shoot live portraits. For how else could their personalities manifest themselves? I wanted to show the curious tilt of the dragonfly's head and its smile, the playfulness of the pill bugs and ants. Some bugs, like the Praying Mantis, posed all day long, and we had long conversations. Some bugs seemed to become hypnotized by the blinding flash of the lights I used, and, as I photographed them, hours zoomed by. When my eyes got tired and I had to quit, I either released the bug or kept it for another angle at a later time. Sometimes I shot an entire roll of one bug, until I felt that I had gotten the best view, the best angle, a particular feature lit up perfectly, an iridescent part shining, a great profile. These are, after all, portraits of bugs.

I have been touched by how willing people have been to help me find bugs, how excited they got when they found a bug that they thought was exceptional. I think they see bugs differently now. I think they slowed down a little, became kids again, and felt the joy of discovery and wonderment.

Most of these bugs are your basic, backyard types. After I had exhausted the bug portrait possibilities around my home, I invited myself to the homes of far-flung friends in southern New Mexico, northern Florida, Shelter Island in New York, and Montana. But the fact that some of these bugs were found in remote areas does not make them exotic or rare. When choosing my subjects, I tried to avoid wildly glamorous bugs. I liked the way rather ordinary bugs became extraordinary when I took the time to really look, up close. Their delicacy, their color, an odd face, or perhaps an antenna thrilled me.

In addition to the peaceful joy this project brought me, I also gained an unexpected and disturbing knowledge. The places I visited in New Mexico, Florida, and Montana have been left alone; they are wild places, free of pesticides, and at each of them, bugs literally flew in the window. But in New York, where humans have tamed nature to make room for their pest-free, cultivated gardens and farms, bugs were few and far between. I was stunned by their comparative scarcity. If you are thinking, "So what?"— well, think again.

Consider the interconnectedness of all living things, including bugs. Consider caterpillars moving across a Polynesian island, denuding trees of their leaves, and in doing so, permitting sunlight to reach the jungle floor, so other plants proliferate. Consider woodpeckers who make sap holes that attract flies and ants, which in turn provide food for their young. In nature, it all seems so neatly planned. Everyone does their job. No one slacks off or takes too much or figures out a way to gather food cheaper or mass-produce it, thereby upsetting the balance. We humans do so at our own peril.

As you look at these photographs, you may find yourself straying from the task of simply looking at the pictures, of looking at these bugs with the eyes of a child. Odd questions may pop into your head, such as "What is the life span of this bug?" or "How many eggs does it lay?" Try to stay with the simple joy of discovery. Later, if you are losing sleep over your question, go to a library, but be forewarned: very little is known about the life cycles of many bugs. After all, how long do any of *us* have? If I tell you that a certain bug has a life span of three months, does this tell the whole story? A predator could eat the eggs. A flood could wipe them out. A parasitic insect could eat the bug. A snake might get it. Or a bird. A person could step on it or run over it. These photographs are not the bugs. They are not their lives. They are a way to get you to look at bugs, and see them differently, that is all.

I hope these portraits inspire you to stop and look at a bug the next time you see one. Its species will probably outlive ours.

A FINAL NOTE ON THE ORGANIZATION OF THIS BOOK: I am a photographer. I am also a sometime decorator and location scout. I am not an entomologist, though I arrogantly thought I might know as much as one when I completed this project. Instead, I have learned how much there is to be learned about bugs and their life cycles, and how much is still unknown. Identifying bugs was much harder than I expected it to be—often I had to seek expert help for positive identification.

Scientists organize the biological world into a series of ever-smaller groups, ending with *species,* collections of like individuals that breed with one another. Different species can be members of the same *genus,* which is the next-smallest grouping in the hierarchy. Scientific names appear in this book as "labels," with the genus given first, then the species.

In the text that accompanies each photograph, I have given each bug's scientific name, though sometimes no species name can be given positively. In some cases, an expert would have had to dissect the bug to identify its genus and species, so for those bugs I have not given a species name. Instead the name is given as "*genus* sp." The abbreviation "sp" stands for the word *species.* Other scientific words used in this book are defined in the glossary.

There is also a separate section following the photographs that gives additional background on the bug families and their different characteristics.

There is no method to my madness in my choice of bugs or their order of appearance in this book. They were photographed and chosen for these pages according to luck, whim, and timing, and their appeal to me at a given moment.

7

The

These Velvet Mites were about one-eighth of an inch long and wide. They are found throughout North America, but I never thought I would find any because they are so small, and so exotically colored. I was looking for arrowheads when I saw several bright, tiny spots on the ground. I carefully picked them up and put them in my bug jar. Each time I checked on them throughout the next few hours (until I got home) they seemed dead. I imagined they must need cow blood or dog blood to live. I thought about using Buster, my dog, to revive them, but I suspected they were just playing dead— which they were. But they do look like they could bite.

I also heard them called water bugs. Some people think that they become drunk on water from the rain and come to the surface from deep underground. It is amazing what people make up about bugs.

10   *Family Trombidiidae*

I have avoided photographing butterflies for years because they are hard to catch, easy to hurt, and do not pose well. But I could not resist this Cloudless Sulphur Butterfly because of its color. Its wingspan was about three inches. It is found mostly in the southern United States, though it sometimes migrates northward. I took a walk one evening on a red clay road and saw thirty dead Cloudless Sulphurs— roadkills. Some of their bodies were being eaten by ants. Their color was intense and beautiful against the umber color of the clay.

Family Pieridae

"Fair even in death! this peerless butterfly."
—THE DUNCIAD, *Alexander Pope*

11

This Fiery Searcher Beetle, or Caterpillar Hunter, was caught in Texas by my sister, who was pregnant and had way too much to do. She forgot about the bug for a month, then sent it to me in a box with some air holes. Two weeks later, when I returned from a trip, I found the box waiting for me, the beetle inside and still alive. After I took its picture, I gave this resilient creature, which can live up to four years, to someone who cares for bugs.

Family Carabidae

"My soul looked back and wondered how I got over."
—SPIRITUAL

Calosoma scrutator

This Dung Fly was in my house, trying to get out the screened window. I noticed that he had red eyes and that he looked greyer and skinnier than other flies. There are more than five hundred species in this family of flies in North America alone. They are found, not surprisingly, near barnyards or animal pastures.

Family Anthomyiidae

Scatophaga sp.

"*A fly is as untamable as a hyena.*"
—*Ralph Waldo Emerson*

14

*"Don't rely too much on labels,
For too often they are fables."*
—SALT CELLARS, *C.H. Spurgeon*

My niece from Texas brought me this Daring
Jumping Spider in a jar. It was only about
half an inch long, and I thought it was rather
dull, just a small black spider—until I saw
its metallic green fangs. It sat very quietly
for its portrait, and it was not until later,
when I looked it up, that I discovered its
name. It could've fooled me.

Family Salticidae   **15**

Dyspteris abortivaria

I was going to bed, exhausted for no good reason. When I reached over to turn out the light, there was this lovely, tiny green moth that seemed to want to have its portrait made. So I got up and took its picture, hoping that would help it get on with its life cycle. This moth, as it turns out, was once an Inchworm.

Family Geometridae   **16**

"*Thus has the candle singed the moth.*
O, these deliberate fools!"
—THE MERCHANT OF VENICE, *William Shakespeare*

18

Polyphylla declimlineata

A friend brought this Ten-lined June Beetle to a restaurant in a cube-shaped brown box with a chic khaki-colored sheer bow on top. I opened the box, thinking it was a gift, and it was a *wonderful* gift. She had given it a twig with leaves, and I added a piece of apricot from dessert. It was about one and one-quarter inches long with these fabulous stripes and a very hairy underside. The Ten-lined June Beetle's habitat is forests and woods in the Rocky Mountain states and the Southwest. The larvae feed on the roots of woody plants, including fruit trees. The adults fly low over fields on warm evenings, sometimes gathering around artificial lights at night. This beetle was shy at first and would not fan out its antennae for some time.

Family Scarabaeidae

19

Pardosa sp.

This Wolf Spider, with her egg sac, was so elegant in her tenaciousness, so regal in her bearing. Her body was about an inch and a half long, her egg sac the size of a nickel. A female Wolf Spider will defend her egg sac with her life. About three weeks after she spins her egg sac around her egg mass, she will bite the sac open and ninety or so spiderlings will emerge, then climb onto her abdomen and stay until they are ready to leave. She is harmless to people.

20 *Family Carabidae*

The Gulf Fritillary Butterfly is in the Brush-footed Butterfly family. It lives in tropical forests and adjacent open areas. Its range is the southern United States from the Atlantic to the Pacific Coasts; it rarely strays northward. The Gulf Fritillary flies all year long in Florida. Both the caterpillars and butterflies contain a poisonous chemical that comes from the passion flower foliage the caterpillars like to eat, hence they have few predators.

Family Nymphalidae

"The velvet nap which on his wings doth lie,
The silken downe with which his backe is dight,
His broad outstretched hornes, his hayrie thies,
His glorious colours, and his glistening eies."
—"MUIOPOTMOS," *Edmund Spenser*

Agraulis vanillae

21

"To-day I saw the Dragon Fly
Come from the wells where he did lie;
An inner impulse rent the veil
Of his old husk; from head to tail
Came out clear plates of sapphire mail.
He dried his wings—like gauze they grew:
Thro' crofts and pastures wet with dew
A living flash of light he flew."
—"THE TWO VOICES,"
Alfred Lord Tennyson

This Red Saddlebag Dragonfly is in the Common Skimmer family. Its wingspan was about three and a half inches. I caught it in northern Florida. It lives in swampy areas, and is a high and fast flyer. Its range is the Southeast and the southern United States all the way to California.

22   *Family Libellulidae*

Citheronia regalis

Who cares what the moth looks like? What a caterpillar! Okay, okay, I didn't find this one in my backyard. I borrowed this Regal Moth Caterpillar, or Hickory Horned Devil, from a man who raises them. We met at night in a parking lot—he showed me this giant, obscenely beautiful caterpillar in the car headlights, holding it casually in his hand. When I took its portrait, it reminded me of a dragon in a Chinese New Year's parade. It was five inches long. The Regal Moth (and Caterpillar) live in deciduous forests in the eastern United States.

Family Saturniidae **23**

Mastigoproctus giganteus

" 'What sort of insects do you rejoice in, where you come from?' the gnat inquired.
" 'I don't rejoice in insects at all,' Alice explained, 'because I'm rather afraid
of them—at least the large kinds. But I can tell you the names of some of them.' "
— THROUGH THE LOOKING GLASS, _Lewis Carroll_

One evening in southern New Mexico, I was doing the floor part of a "Jane Fonda" routine—specifically the push-ups. I was almost finished when I looked up and found myself face-to-face with this Giant Vinegarone. I honestly can't remember if I finished the push-ups. But I did the stretching exercises after I caught him in a small basket that was nearby. He was four inches long, not including his whip, or tail.

25   *Family Thelyphonidae*

This Carpenter Bee was hovering around a plant on Shelter Island, New York. Their range is the eastern United States. The female chews a tunnel in the dry wood of lumber, dead trees, or houses, making a linear series of unlined cells divided by wood chips. She provisions each with pollen and nectar before laying one egg in each cell. To emerge, adults wait in line to the end of the tunnel for their turn to leave, like human commuters.

Family Anthophoridae

*"Instead of dirt and poison we have rather chosen to fill our hives
with honey and wax; thus furnishing mankind with the two noblest of things,
which are sweetness and light."*
—BATTLE OF THE BOOKS, *Jonathan Swift*

Armadillidium vulgare

My sisters and I called them rolybugs when we were little. I have heard them called roly-poly bugs, doodle bugs, pill bugs, sow bugs, even baseball bugs. They curl into a tight ball for defense or to reduce water loss, much like the extinct trilobites. I found these under a poppy plant, and put them back when I was through.

Class Crustacea
ORDER ISOPODA

"A man need not know how to name all the oaks or the moths, or be able to recognize a synclinal fault, or tell time by the stars, in order to possess Nature. He may have his mind solely on growing larkspurs, or he may love a boat and a sail and a blue-eyed day at sea. He may have a bent for making paths or banding birds, or he may be only an inveterate and curious walker."
—AN ALMANAC FOR MODERNS, *Donald Culross Peattie*

28

The Carolina Locust is a Short-horned Grasshopper. It lives on roadsides and dry fields
throughout North America. It eats grasses and
other herbaceous plants, and sometimes beans.
The locust in this picture made a lot of noise, but
only in flight, like some babies on airplanes. I
liked it because its color was monotone. It was
a study in beige. Even its eyes are beige. The
Carolina Locust is like the desert; it can look
boring until you begin to appreciate its subtleties.
I think of it as the Calvin Klein of the insect world.

Family Acrididae

29

Misumena vatia

"When we lose our innocence—when we start feeling the weight of the atmosphere and learn that there's death in the pot—we take leave of our senses. Only children can hear the song of the male house mouse. Only children keep their eyes open. The only thing they have got is sense; they have highly developed "input systems," admitting all data indiscriminately. . . . All my adult life I have wished to see the cemented case of a caddisfly larva. It took . . . the young daughter of friends to find one on the pebbled bottom of a shallow stream on whose bank we sat side by side. "What's that?" she asked. That, I wanted to say as I recognized the prize she held, is a memento mori for people who read too much."

—PILGRIM AT TINKER CREEK, *Annie Dillard*

The Goldenrod Spider, Flower Spider, or Red-spotted Crab Spider is from the Crab Spider family. It can be found throughout North America, on daisies, goldenrod, or other yellow or white flowers. It eats the insects that visit these flowers. The female spins a silken sac for her eggs, but frequently dies before the spiderlings hatch. This spider was brought to me with the flower upon which she was found. She was the size of a pea.

Family Thomisidae

Leucauge mabelae

The tiny Mabel Orchard Spider is a member of the Large-jawed Orb Weaver family. This one's body was a quarter of an inch long. It was in a tree in front of a house in northern Florida. I thought its body was more photogenic than its "large" (all but microscopic) jaws. It lives on the edges of woods and in shrubby meadows. Its range is the eastern United States, and west to Texas and Nebraska.

Family Tetragnathidae

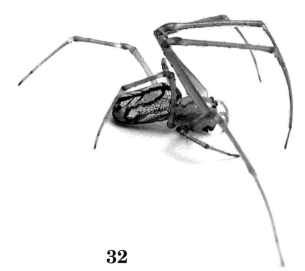

*"Sunshine and summer heat, without
the accompaniment of the cicada's song, or
the quivering of the air, is like a
dance without music."*
—PENSÉES ·J. Joubert

Platypedia sp.

Cicadas are sometimes mistakenly called locusts. I was outside my house in northern New Mexico, at the very beginning of summer, when I heard a slow clacking sound that I had never noticed before. I got as close as I could to a mountain mahogany tree, scanned it for a long time (maybe ninety seconds), and encountered this cicada. The males, to attract females, make noises with sound-producing organs, called tymbals, on their abdomens. The membraneous tymbals are buckled, then flattened, like a tin lid, by contracting a muscle. Each movement makes a click, and a series of clicks makes the sometimes maddening sound one associates with hot summer days.

This Giant Desert Millipede was six inches long and seemed to me more closely related to a crustacean than a bug. A friend's kids keep them as pets. They make doo-doos bigger than mice. It did not take me long to shoot him. This creature is so without endearing qualities, that I can't even think of anything nice to say, except that he is harmless and eats plants.

CLASS DIPLOPODA

Family Spirostreptidae

Orthoporus ornatus

This Tiger Moth, with his owl-like face, was trying to get in my house one night, attracted by the light. I liked his hair-do. I liked him even more when I saw the pink markings on his legs and his body that he seemed so reluctant to show me.

Family Arctiidae

Hemihyalca sp.

"Every association of moths is with night and mystery and death."
—AN ALMANAC FOR MODERNS,
Donald Culross Peattie

Daddy longlegs are not really spiders, though they are Arachnids. Their legs break off easily and cannot be regenerated. They are nocturnal and they eat other insects, other daddy longlegs, snails, aphids, and earthworms. Light as a feather and practically invisible, he still casts a shadow.

Family Phalangiidae

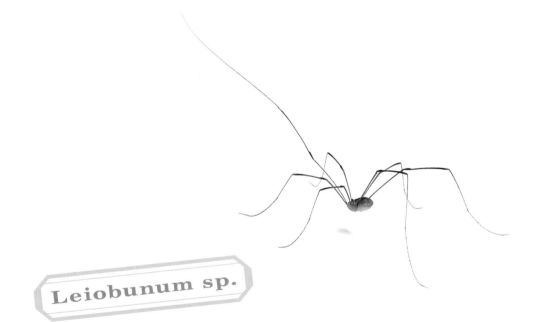

Leiobunum sp.

"They were singing on this planet before us;
they will sing after us, celebrating what can
never change, the fiery glory of the sun."
—THE WONDERS OF INSTINCT, *Jean Henri Fabre*

Eremobates pallipes

I saw this Pale Windscorpion out of the corner of my eye as I was heading to bed one night in southern New Mexico. It was hard to catch, and I was not sure what it was or if it could sting me. It ran so fast that I had to wait until someone could help me wrangle it into place and shoot it. The only way we could slow it down enough to take its picture was to blow a whiff of cigarette smoke into the bug jar.

Family Eremobatidae

Romalea microptera

My friends called them crickets
and they said they were big, but I'd
have had a heart attack if they hadn't warned me.
This creature is no cricket, it's a Southeastern Lubber
Grasshopper, and I found it within five minutes of
going outside on my first morning in northern
Florida. They were everywhere, usually in twos,
stacked vertically. I saw some that were almost four
inches long, but despite their size, Lubber Grasshoppers are quite docile and easy to catch. Their range
is the southeastern United States, west to Louisiana,
and northeast to Tennessee. They eat herbaceous
plants, any old kind. Adults come
out in June and live until November.
They cannot fly, which produces a
somewhat sedentary lifestyle that
lends itself to sex addiction.

Family Acrididae

39

The Green June Beetle is in the Scarab Beetle family. Years ago my mother sent me some of these beetles, overnight, in a package with large breathing holes, but when the box arrived, it was empty. I can only guess that the beetles escaped through the holes into the delivery van. The June Beetles in this picture were sent to me from Texas in a box with a single Rice Crispy. I gave them all a quick shower in the kitchen sink, put some peanut oil on their parched wing covers, and fed them fresh peach pieces. They were about three-quarters of an inch long. Green June Beetles live in gardens, orchards, open woods, and crop fields in the southeastern United States and the Gulf States, to Missouri. They drink pollen and eat fruit—they are especially partial to peaches. Their larvae eat the roots of grasses, alfalfa, tobacco, and many other plants.

In Egypt, about 600 B.C., a carved image of the Scarab Beetle (today identified as the Dung Beetle, in the Scarab family) was placed next to the heart in a mummified body. The flat side of the Scarab was always inscribed with a spell from the Book of the Dead, to prevent the heart from testifying against its owner during the postmortem "weighing of the heart" before the divine judges. The Scarab Beetle was also a symbol of resurrection, and the sun. Nowadays, they are thought to bring good luck.

Family Scarabaeidae

Cotinus nitida

40

41

Pogonomyrmex rugosus

"Go to the ant, thou sluggard; consider her ways, and be wise."

—PROVERBS, 6:6

42

I found these Harvester Ants in northern New
Mexico, at my house. They're the ants that make
hills and circular mounds layered with pebbles.
The pebbles conduct heat into the hill to warm
the eggs that are just below the surface. Harvester
Ant nests can be ten feet deep, and can hold as
many as twelve thousand ants. The ants mind
their own business unless disturbed—then they
defend their colony by stinging.

43   *Family Formicidae*

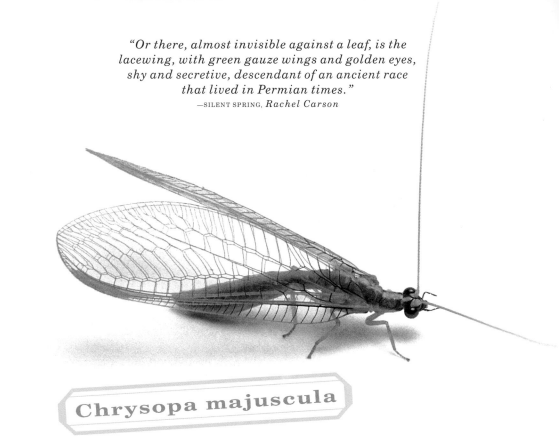

"Or there, almost invisible against a leaf, is the lacewing, with green gauze wings and golden eyes, shy and secretive, descendant of an ancient race that lived in Permian times."
—SILENT SPRING, *Rachel Carson*

Chrysopa majuscula

This Green Lacewing's body was about one-half inch long. I found it drowning in a barrel that collects rainwater from my roof. It is common throughout North America, and lives near forests, in meadows, and in gardens. California Green Lacewings are raised for use in greenhouses and vineyards—they eat mealybugs. Only a specialist can identify the dozens of species.

Family Chrysopidae

44

Ceuthophilus pallidus

I found this Camel Cricket on the gate to a place where I'd like to live someday, a faraway place that needs a new house and a person like me who has dogs. Camel Crickets are nocturnal and live in dark places, like caves or basements. Something brought this one out of a hole in the gate post into the light of day. I think it was an omen. The sun was blistering hot, and nothing else was stirring. My key fit the lock on the gate, and a breeze came up. As I was leaving and locking the gate, I had that good feeling one gets when one has a place to go, a plan, an option.

Family Gryllacrididae

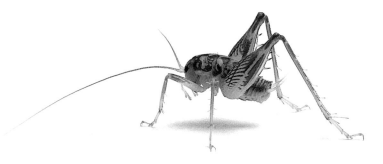

Cicindela sp.

Tiger Beetles are usually shiny and metallic, ranging from three-eighths to seven-eighths of an inch long. Most are diurnal. These long-legged, fast runners are predators, using their powerful jaws to seize and kill smaller insects. I found this little Tiger Beetle hopping down a road in Montana after losing the biggest trout I ever had on a fly rod, after a perfect cast, which hooked me on the sport for life.

46   *Family Cicindelidae*

The Mourning Cloak Butterfly reminds me of bark or wrinkled fabric. It lives in woods, meadows, and suburban and urban parks throughout North America. I found this one in Montana. It was about two inches tall.

The caterpillars are considered pests because they often defoliate willow, elm, and poplar trees.

Family Nymphalidae

"And, what's a butterfly? At best,
He's but a caterpillar drest;"
—THE BUTTERFLY AND THE SNAIL,
Gary Romain

Pachydiplax longipennis

This Swift Long-winged Skimmer
Dragonfly was circling a roadside pond
in southern New Mexico. The species is
found throughout North America and
eats small insects. Its body was one and
a half inches long. He was friendly and
cooperative, always quick with a smile.
It took me five minutes to do his portrait.
He was not fussy or vain about his hair.

Family Libellulidae

49

"Dost thou not know we Worms are born, Angelic Butterflies to form?"
—QUOTED IN BOOK OF NATURE, *Jan Swammerdam*

50

Calephelis sp.

"Cousin Itt," the larval form of a Metalmark Butterfly, took a long time to photograph—"Itt" was very shy. The lights made it hide its face.

Family Riodinidae

The Cow Killer Wasp is in the oddly named Velvet Ant family of wasps. Their range is the southeastern United States and the Gulf coast. The females, which are wingless, lay one egg beside each cell, where the egg of a bee has been left to develop. When hatched, the larvae invade the cells, feeding on and killing the bee larvae. The Cow Killer larvae then complete their metamorphosis in their victim's brood cells. Cow Killers run fast, and deliver a sting so painful "it could kill a cow."

Family Mutillidae

Dasymutilla occidentalis

53

I named this bug Beetlejuice, though its common name is the Striped Blister Beetle. The larvae sometimes eat grasshopper eggs, while the adults eat potatoes, beets, and alfalfa. Friends brought this bug to me in a shoe box and gave it to me in exchange for a portrait of their dog, Jinx.

Family Meloidae

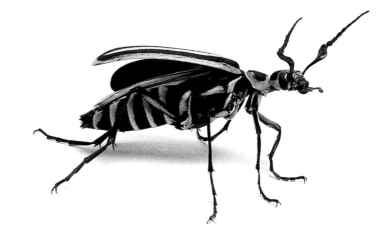

"And the poor beetle, that we tread upon,
In corporal sufferance finds a pang as great
As when a giant dies."
—MEASURE FOR MEASURE, *William Shakespeare*

One morning, while trying unsuccessfully to catch a fish for lunch, I noticed five or six orange dragonflies, and many huge black, green and blue dragonflies flying all around. I quit fishing, walked into the water, and waited for an orange one to land near me, because I had read that dragonflies always take off forwards at a forty-five-degree angle. Not true.

I swished this Red Skimmer Dragonfly right out of the air. Its body was about two inches long, its wingspan about three. These dragonflies live from Kansas to California, south to Mexico, and north to Montana. The adults eat small insects, especially mosquitos, that they catch in flight.

You can see its eye on its tilted head, looking up at the camera. Check out the goofy smile.

Family Libellulidae

"If you wish to live and thrive,
Let the spider run alive."
—OLD SAYING

56

Gasteracantha elipsoides

This Crablike Spiny Orb Weaver Spider was about one-half inch across. I found her in an azalea tree in northern Florida. These tiny spiders live on the edges of woodlands and in shrubby gardens. Their range extends from the southeastern United States west to California. They eat the small insects that they catch in round, vertical webs that they weave anew each night. The male is even smaller than the female and is seldom noticed, unlike most males in the animal kingdom.

Family Araneidae　　　**57**

Nephila clavipes

The Golden-silk Spider, also known as the Calico Spider, is in the Orb Weaver family. It lives in shaded woodlands and swamps in the southeastern United States. Including the legs, this spider was as big as my hand. I had heard about its ferocious bite and was nervously careful when riding horses along paths spanned by its webs. Golden-silk Spider webs are two to three feet across.

Family Araneidae

" 'Will you walk into my parlor?' said the spider to a fly;
'It's the prettiest little parlor that you ever did spy.' "
—"THE SPIDER AND THE FLY," *Mary Howitt*

This immature California Mantis came in my window in southern New Mexico. He was a little over an inch long. I put him outside, but he came back, so I fed him live moths for a few days, which he snatched from my fingers. I talked to him. I last saw him hanging upside down from the lamp on my desk. Maybe the lizard that I couldn't catch ate him.

Family Mantidae

Stagmomantis californica

"Clinging to the screen
Her graceful feelers
Surveyed his dried remains
She and her baby
Day after day mourning the body
Dragging it fractions of an inch

For a month I watched
And felt sorry
Sorry for the thought
Of ever being left
Sorry for being vulnerable
Sick at the thought of death

Little did I know
She was eating her lover
Had bitten off his head
To feel his strongest thrust
Surge within her
How often I deceive myself."
—"CHEEK TO CHEEK,"
Jo Harvey Allen

61

This Tarantula Hawk Wasp was about one and a quarter inches long. It was caught by a friend, and brought to me at a saloon where we danced the two step for an hour or so, while it waited

Hemipepsis sp.

to be taken home and photographed. Females prey on spiders as food for their larvae. Adults can sting. This species lives on dry hillsides and rolling arid plains. Its range is California and Mexico. Even though Tarantula Hawks are primarily a tropical species, several occur in the Southwest.

Family Pompilidae

This little dinosaur-like creature seemed blinded by my shooting light. It is probably the larva of a Golden Net-wing Beetle, which proliferated in the area in southern New Mexico where I found it. Three-quarters of an inch long, it looked quite prehistoric, totally uncivilized and slow.

Family Lycidae

"The flesh is weary, alas, and I've read all the books."
—*Stéphane Mallarmé*

Lycostomus loripes

63

64

> *"I would not enter on my list of friends*
> *(Though graced with polished manners*
> *and fine sense,*
> *Yet wanting sensibility), the man*
> *Who needlessly sets foot upon a worm."*
>
> —THE TASK, BOOK VI, "WINTER WALK AT NOON,"
> *William Cowper*

Manduca Quinquemaculata

I found this Tomato Hornworm Caterpillar in northern New Mexico. He is a member of the Sphinx Moth family. I wanted to keep him and watch his development until he turned into the next thing but he was a messy houseguest. I turned him loose on my very own plants, in gratitude for his portrait.

Family Sphingidae

Scientific

background

One of the biggest phyla in the animal kingdom is *Phylum Arthropoda*. All bugs are arthropods, and they all have an exoskeleton and segmented bodies. The classes of arthropods pictured in this book are *Class Crustacea,* including pillbugs; *Class Diplopoda,* with millipedes; and, of course, spiders. *Arachnids* lack antennae, have eight legs, and their bodies have two distinct parts, the cephalothorax, and the abdomen.

Also pictured in this book are members of *Class Insecta,* the largest and most familiar class in the phylum *Arthropoda.* It has about one hundred thousand species in North America. Like other arthropods, Insects have exoskeletons, and segmented bodies, but unlike spiders, for example, or pillbugs, Insects' bodies have three parts: a head with antennae, a thorax with three pairs of jointed legs and wings, and an abdomen.

Insects can further be distinguished from other *Arthropoda* because they grow by shedding their exoskeletons, in a series of molts. As they grow, they change in form in a process known as metamorphosis. There are two kinds of metamorphosis: simple and complete. In simple metamorphosis, the immature insects (called nymphs) resemble the adults, except they are smaller and have no wings. They live in the same habitat and generally eat the same things that adults do. In complete metamorphosis, insect eggs hatch into larvae that do not resemble the adult. Larvae pass through several stages of development, finally becoming pupae. Pupae are usually inactive and nonfeeding, and they may be in a cocoon. In the pupal stage, metamorphosis takes place. *Class Insecta* bugs that appear in this book are dragonflies, katydids, crickets, cicadas, lacewings, beetles, butterflies and moths, flies, ants, wasps, bees, and mantids.

PHYLUM ARTHROPODA *Class Diplopoda*

FAMILY SPIROSTREPTIDAE, the Millipedes, are found from the poles to the tropics, including in deserts. They are detritivores, meaning they eat mineral and organic debris. They burrow in soil and leaf litter, migrating vertically to control the humidity and temperature of their environment. Millipedes have two pairs of legs on each segment of their bodies, and two glands on each segment that contain a bad-smelling brown fluid the millipede releases when disturbed. They vary widely in size, from tiny and flat to lengths in excess of ten inches.

PHYLUM ARTHROPODA *Class Crustacea*

Order Isopoda, of which the pillbugs are members, are bugs that live in dark, damp places. They are important contributors to the process of breaking down dead plant material.

PHYLUM ARTHROPODA *Class Arachnida*

Order Araneae, the spiders are the largest group within *Class Arachnida*. They are also the largest group of Arthropods that are not insects—there are three thousand species of spiders in North America. Most have eight simple eyes and venom glands and fangs to paralyze prey. Young spiders, and some adult males, swing from place to place on long strands from their spinnerets, or silk making glands. This is called ballooning. Most females lay eggs in sacs made of silk. Some attach the sac to the web or twigs. Some carry it around until the eggs hatch. Spiderlings occasionally eat each other. All spiders are considered beneficial because they eat so many insects.

The spiders in the FAMILY TETRAGNATHIDAE, or Large-jawed Orb Weavers, have unusually large jaws or chelicerae. There are around twenty five species in North America. They eat small insects. To wait for prey, they hang below the web, holding on to a single strand of silk with one leg. Orchard spiders can be distinguished from other large-jawed spiders by the plate that protects the opening of the female sex organs.

The FAMILY ARANEIDAE, the Orb Weavers, have several hundred species in North America. These spiders have eight eyes in two rows. Most spin the familiar spiraling web built on support lines radiating from the center. Many replace the entire web every day.

FAMILY LYCOSIDAE, or Wolf Spiders, have eight eyes arranged in three rows. Most live on the ground and are active nocturnal hunters with sharp vision. Most do not weave webs and most do not build shelters. The female spins her egg, attaches to her spinnerets, and keeps it with her until the spiderlings hatch. There are over one hundred species of Thin-legged Wolf Spiders in the United States and Canada, distinguishable by specialists only.

FAMILY SALTICIDAE include Jumping Spiders. The Daring Jumping Spider's range is from the Atlantic coast to the Rocky Mountains. It eats insects, and jumps away if the female approaches too rapidly in courting. Most of the Crab Spiders in the FAMILY THOMISIDAE hold their legs out to the sides and can walk in any direction, like a crab. They range in size from

67

one-sixteenth of an inch to three-eighths of an inch. There are more than two hundred North American species. The male of certain species sometimes tie the female down before mating. The females produce an egg mass late in the year, then die. The eggs overwinter, then spiderlings hatch and disperse in the spring.

Order Acarina are mites and ticks. There are about one thousand named species of ticks and thirty thousand known species of mites worldwide. Most are small, from one-sixty-fourth of an inch to one inch long. Many mites are beneficial, preying on the eggs of aphids, plant-eating insects, and roundworms. Most ticks are parasites and carry diseases. I did not see any ticks, I am happy to say, in all my travels. Even if I had, they are not photogenic.

The Velvet Mites of FAMILY TROMBIDIIDAE are red and covered with hair. Adults eat insect eggs. The larvae, called Red Bugs, are parasites of insects, spiders, daddy long legs, and Scorpions. They are found in most woods and deserts.

Order Solpugida, consisting of Windscorpions with a pair of pincer like chelicerae, number one hundred twenty species in North America. They have two eyes at the front margin of the cephalothoracic area, a three-part thorax, and a ten-part abdomen. The mouthparts are used independently of each other: one pair holds the prey, the other cuts it. The Windscorpion's long pedipalps carry water to the mouth. They are also held like, and perform as, feelers. Most Windscorpions live in dry regions, but some live in the mountains. They eat small insects and lizards. They are fast runners (that is how they got their name). Most are nocturnal. Their range is from Arizona to North Dakota.

FAMILY EREMOBATIDAE are most of the North American Windscorpions. They use their poisonless pincers to subdue their prey.

Order Uropygi, or Whipscorpions, have a long, whiplike tail instead of a stinger. During the day, they hide under logs and rotting wood or in humid, dark corners indoors. At night they hunt for small insects. These arachnids have two heavy pincerlike pedipalps and four pairs of legs. The first pair is used for feelers. Nocturnal predators, Whipscorpions use their tails to distribute a defensive secretion that contains acetic acid or vinegar. They do not have poison glands, so they are not harmful to people. Whipscorpions are mostly tropical arachnids; there is only one species in North America, in the Southwest.

The Vinegarones are in the FAMILY THELYPHONIDAE. They have eight eyes, two in the middle and three one each side of the head, and they can really pinch. They are the only family of Whipscorpions in North America.

Order Opiliones, the daddy longlegs, are not spiders, though they are Arachnids. The Latin word *opilio* means shepherd, the long legs reminiscent of the stilts shepherds used to walk about on when counting sheep. The legs of those fragile creatures break off easily and cannot be regenerated. Daddy longlegs have two eyes on a raised turret at the middle of the cephalothorax, one on the right and one on the left. Males and females do not perform elaborate mating rituals, they simply touch each other with their legs. Most species live for about a year. They are nocturnal, and they eat insects, other daddy longlegs, snails, aphids, and earthworms. The two hundred species in North America are in the FAMILY PHALANGIIDAE. In England, daddy longlegs are called Harvestmen and in France, Reapers.

PHYLUM ARTHROPODA *Class Insecta*

Order Coleoptera, the beetles, are the largest and most successful order in the animal kingdom. They constitute one-third of all insects—thirty thousand species in North America alone. They range in size from one-sixteenth of an inch to five inches in length. Some fly, some crawl, some swim. They all have the elytra, the forewings that cover the hind wings (that are for flying). They have chewing mouthparts and eat a variety of foods. Some are predators, some are parasites. Metamorphosis is complete, so the larvae (called grubs) do not look like the adults. They transform during a pupal stage. Some beetles attack plants or stored foods, others pollinate flowers and eat plant pests. Some are good scavengers, some are bad pests.

FAMILY CICINDELIDAE, or Tiger Beetles, are usually shiny and metallic-looking, ranging from three-eighths to seven-eighths of an inch long. Most are diurnal, long legged, and fast runners. They are predators who use their powerful jaws to seize and kill smaller insects.

FAMILY CARABIDAE, or Ground Beetles, are represented by over three thousand species in North America. They are one-eighth to one and three-eighths inches long. Most pursue prey at night. Adults can live up to four years. The species that eat only caterpillars are thought to be beneficial.

FAMILY SCARABAEIDAE are the scarab beetles. Usually brightly colored, they have large heads, and measure one-fourth to two and three-eighths inches in length. They have clubbed antennae composed of leaflike plates, called lamellae, that can be held together or fanned out to sense odors. Both adults and larvae are nocturnal. Many are important scavengers that recycle carrion and other decaying matter. Some are agricultural pests. There are about thirteen hundred species in North America.

FAMILY MELOIDAE, or Blister Beetles, contain cantharidin, a chemical that can cause blisters on human skin. Their bodies are elongated, from three-eighths to one and one-eighth inches long. They are plant eaters, though some larvae eat grasshopper eggs. A few dried beetles mixed in with horses' hay or alfalfa can cause colic.

FAMILY LYCIDAE are the net-veined beetles. They are small and resemble fireflies—they are usually red or yellow with bulging eyes. Adults live off of plant juices or small insects; the larva eat insects. The Golden Netwing's range is throughout Arizona and New Mexico at low elevations.

Order Diptera account for more than sixteen thousand species of flies in North America. They only have one pair of wings, the second pair having evolved into little knobby things (halteres). Halteres help flies stabilize flight and orient themselves in space. They have relatively large eyes. Flies exhibit complete metamorphosis, and their larvae are called maggots. Since most flies are scavengers, they are extremely important in the process of decomposition, and in recycling nutrients through an ecosystem. Some flies carry diseases, some carry bacteria. Others are agricultural pests. On the positive side, some flies are flower pollinators, some are food for other wildlife, and some help control other insect pests. Identification is tricky because it comes down to differentiating between fine anatomical features like bristles, wing veination, and genital structure.

FAMILY ANTHOMYIIDAE, or the Anthomyiid Flies, closely resemble house flies but are more slight. Their larvae feed on plant tissues. Some breed in dung or other decaying matter.

Order Hymenoptera include more than seventeen thousand species of bees, ants, wasps, and sawflies in North America. They usually have two pairs of wings. All have chewing mouthparts and some have tongue-like parts for ingesting liquids. Females of most species have an ovipositor—in some species, the ovipositor has been modified into a stinger. Metamorphosis is complete, with four distinct growing stages: egg, larva, pupa, adult. The larva is an active feeding stage, and the pupa is an inactive resting stage when the larva transforms into the adult. Some species of sawflies damage trees and crops, but parasitic species help to control some insect pests. Bees and some wasps act as pollinators of crops and wild plants.

Velvet ants, FAMILY MUTILLIDAE, are densely hairy wasps such as the Cow Killer Wasp. They are usually red, yellow, or orange. The females lack wings. Adults live on nectar and water; larvae feed on the larvae and pupae of other wasps, bees, flies, and beetles.

Ants are in the FAMILY FORMICIDAE. Most have a complex social structure with two castes of sterile females and a reproductive cast of winged fertile males and females. They live in colonies underground or in dead wood. Most species are predators or scavengers; some harvest seeds.

Spider Wasps, in the FAMILY POMPILIDAE, are largish wasps with some species reaching lengths of up to two inches. Adults drink nectar from flowers. Females of many species prey on Tarantulas and Trapdoor Spiders, using them for food for their larvae. The female stings the spider between the legs, immobilizing it. She then quickly digs a burial chamber, drags the spider inside, deposits a single egg on it, and closes the burrow. When hatched, the wasp larvae feeds on the imprisoned spider, eventually killing it. A few species of Spider Wasps are nest parasites, laying their eggs in the provisioned eggs of other Spider Wasps.

Carpenter Bees, members of the ANTHOPHORIDAE FAMILY, are sturdy looking and less hairy than bumblebees. They are often black with a bluish iridescence. Experts look at the veins in the wings of Anthophorid bees to distinguish them from members of other bee families.

Order Lepidoptera includes moths and butterflies. They have four wings covered with delicate pigmented or prismatic scales that rub off easily. There are twelve thousand species in North America. Wingspans vary from one-eighth inch to ten inches. The mouthparts consist of a long, hollow, coiled tube, or proboscis, for drinking nectar or tree sap. Butterflies fly during the day, and most hold their wings together vertically when they are at rest. Most moths fly at night, are less brightly colored than butterflies, and hold their wings tentlike over their bodies, curled around the body, or flat when resting. Metamorphosis is complete. The larvae, called caterpillars, have well-developed heads with strong jaws and functional legs. They feed on plants. The pupa of a moth may have a cocoon. The pupa of a butterfly does not. Some moths and butterflies are agricultural pests, though most are harmless. Some are valuable as pollinators of flowers or as a source of commercial silk.

The FAMILY PIERIDAE are the Whites, Sulphurs, and Orange Tips—the most familiar butterflies. Members of this family have full-sized forelegs for walking and rounded wings. Their wingspans range from seven-eighths of an inch to two and three-quarters inches. Their antennae end in a clublike structure. The FAMILY NYMPHALIDAE, or Brush-Footed Butterflies, are butterflies with very small forelegs, long, hairy scales on the wings, and wingspans from one to four inches. The males in this family sometimes drench the female in an aphrodisiac scent when mating.

FAMILY RIODINIDAE are the Metalmark Butterflies. They are smallish, with beautiful metallic markings. The long hairs of the larvae serve as an irritant to whoever might be so unlucky as to eat one.

The FAMILY SATURNIIDAE include the Giant Silkworm Moths, with wingspans from one to almost six inches. They do not have hearing organs. The adults have very short life spans and do not feed at all—they live to reproduce. Most species overwinter as pupae; some in cocoons, some in earthen chambers. They are the largest moths, and though they are related to the Asiatic Silkworm, these Giant Silkworms do not produce commercially viable silk.

Sphinx Moths, in the FAMILY SPHINGIDAE, beat their wings so rapidly that they resemble hummingbirds. Like the Saturniidae Moths, they cannot hear. The caterpillars are often bright green and have a horn.

FAMILY GEOMETRIDAE, or Measuringworm Moths, are delicate and always hold their wings outstretched, rather than over the body, when at rest. The larvae are called inchworms and can be seen hanging by a strand of silk from foliage.

Tiger Moths, in the FAMILY ARCTIIDAE, are furry and, usually, light colored with bright accent colors. These conspicuous patterns can warn predators of the moth's toxicity. Adults usually do not feed.

Order Orthoptera, consisting of grasshoppers and crickets, are characterized by enlarged hind legs for jumping and large mouthparts for chewing. They have two pairs of wings, though only the hind wings are used for flying. Most females have long ovipositors for depositing eggs in plant stems or underground. Metamorphosis is simple. The males are well known for the sounds they make by rubbing their wings or legs together. These sounds can be forewarning, courtship, or establishing territory. There are about one thousand species in North America.

Family Acrididae, the Short-horned Grasshoppers, have short, horn-shaped antennae. You can see their hearing organs—round, flat, tympana on each side of the first abdominal segment of the body. They make a buzzing sound by creating friction between a ridge on the inside of the hind leg and one or more veins on the forewing. The females lay eggs underground, usually hatching in the summer. The Acrididae Grasshoppers are fairly common. Some species are called locusts, from locusta, the Latin word for grasshopper.

Family Gryllacrididae are comprised of Camel Crickets and their kin. They have humped tan or gray bodies and very large hind femora. Their thin antennae are often longer than their bodies. Most males do not make sounds and both sexes lack tympana and good eyesight, relying on their long antennae to feel their way around. Most also lack wings. All are nocturnal and live in dark caves, basements, or under wood or rocks.

Order Mantodea, the Mantids, have mobile, triangular heads on a flexible neck. They have prominent compound eyes, strong mouthparts to cut through the armored shells of insects, and very thin antennae. Their forelegs are adapted for grasping prey, which, for the female Mantids, can mean the males of their own species—the female sometimes devours the male during mating. One explanation of this is that the male mates more effectively when its head (usually the first thing to go) has been eaten. Freed from control by the brain, the male's genitalia can respond with incessant copulatory movements. In the fall, females lay hundreds of eggs, attaching them to twigs in foamy masses. The foam hardens, and protects the eggs from birds. In spring, soft, light-colored nymphs come out and, through simple metamorphosis, quickly unfold into tiny Mantids. The young start eating small insects and, sometimes, each other. There are eleven species in North America, all considered to be very beneficial because they eat so many smaller pest insects.

Family Mantidae includes all the Mantids, who use their slender middle and hind legs for walking and jumping.

Order Homoptera, which include Cicadas and their kin, have six thousand species in North America. They are all plant feeders. Metamorphosis is simple.

Family Cicadidae, or Cicadas, are fairly large insects, up to two and one-half inches long. Sometimes mistakenly called locusts, Cicadas are not jumping insects, like Grasshoppers. They spend up to fourteen years in a nymph stage underground, feeding on roots of trees that they climb eventually, shedding their skin and molting into adults. Their empty nymphal skins can be seen by the hundreds, hanging from trees in July and August, after the adults have emerged. Each species has a singular song, sometimes a buzz, sometimes a clacking sound.

Order Neuroptera, the Net-Veined Insects, have four wings with very fine veination. There are over three hundred species in North America. They have chewing mouthparts and, usually, large compound eyes. Their larvae go through complete metamorphosis. These insects are considered beneficial because they eat destructive insects.

Green Lacewings, in the FAMILY CHRYSOPIDAE, are very common. All are under an inch long and have prominent, green eyes. The larvae eat aphids and other insects. Pupation takes place in silken cocoons attached to plants. The adults fly at night. To avoid being preyed upon by bats, Green Lacewings have hearing organs in their wing veins that sense the high frequency sounds bats emit.

Order Odonata, Dragonflies and Damselflies, have been around for three hundred million years. Dragonflies once had wingspans of two feet, and today they are still fairly large, with wingspans from one to five inches. There are four hundred fifty species of Dragonflies in North America. All Dragonflies have evolved into specialized hunters, using their movable heads, sharp, cutting mouthparts, large compound eyes, four independently moving wings, and grasping legs to catch and eat midges and mosquitoes. They mate in flight and can fly both forward and backward. Metamorphosis is simple, even though the young (naiads) do not closely resemble the adults.

FAMILY LIBELLULIDAE are the common Skimmer Dragonflies and make up a large part of the Order. They usually have brightly-colored bodies which are noticeably shorter than their wingspans, which can be up to four inches long. The wings often have bands or spots on them. Skimmer Dragonflies' large eyes touch one another at the top of the head.

glossary

abdomen: the last section of a bug's body.

cephalothorax: the first part of a spider's body, made up of the head and thorax.

chelicerae: the first pair of appendages below the cephalothorax of spiders, scorpions, mites, ticks, daddy longlegs, Whipscorpions, and Windscorpions, made up of a first segment and a fang.

chrysalis: the naked pupa of a butterfly.

cocoon: a silk case made by a larva, in which it pupates.

compound eye: a visual organ made up of lots of light-sensitive parts, arrayed with facets (exposed lenses) that fit together.

diurnal: in the daytime.

elytron *(plural, elytra)*: the cover of a beetle's hind wing.

exoskeleton: the supportive structure of a body on the outside, instead of the inside like ours.

femur *(plural, femora)*: the third segment of an insect's leg.

mandible: a jaw of an insect, for chewing.

molt: the shedding of the exoskeleton to allow growth.

naiad: the aquatic young of dragonflies.

nymph: the terrestrial young of insects with simple metamorphosis.

overwinter: to have a period of dormancy in the cold season.

ovipositor: the egg-laying organ at the end of a female's abdomen.

pedipalp: the second appendage on the cephalothorax of spiders, scorpions, mites, ticks, daddy longlegs, Whipscorpions, and Windscorpions. It is a leg for females and a mover of sperm in males; it is used to guide prey to the mouth in both sexes.

pupa: the inactive stage of insect metamorphosis, when the larva has taken its adult form.

spinneret: the appendage below a spider's abdomen that silk comes from.

thorax: the part of the body between the head and abdomen; it has three segments that carry the legs and wings.

tympana: hearing organs.

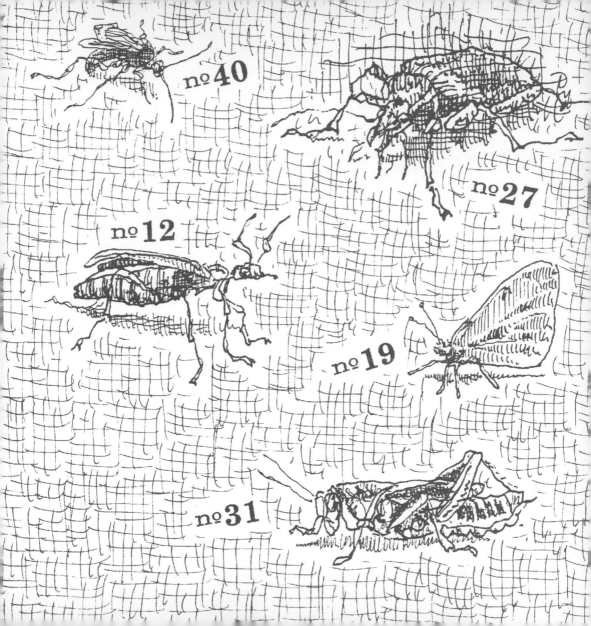